Dream Dogs

NUGGET

With special thanks to Lucy Courtenay and Nellie Ryan

First published in Great Britain by HarperCollins *Children's Books* 2010
HarperCollins Children's Books is a division of HarperCollins*Publishers* Ltd,
77-85 Fulham Palace Road, Hammersmith, London W6 8JB

The HarperCollins *Children's Books* website address is
www.harpercollins.co.uk

I

Dream Dogs : Nugget
Text copyright © HarperCollins 2010
Illustration copyright © HarperCollins 2010

ISBN-13 978 0 00 732036-3

Printed and bound in England by
Clays Ltd, St Ives plc

Dream Dogs

NUGGET

Aimee Harper

HarperCollins *Children's Books*

Special thanks to

The Happy Dog Grooming Parlour, Farnham

Introducing...

Name: Nugget

Breed: golden retriever

Age: 3

Colour: mud brown – to start with…

Likes: Barney the golden retriever

Dislikes: being on a lead

Most likely to be mistaken for: a mud monster

Least likely to be mistaken for: a show dog!

One

Mud Monster

"Over here, Louie!" Bella shouted.

Across Chestnut Park, Bella's little brother bent back his arm to throw the ball. Bella ran backwards, reaching up with her hands. Suddenly she stumbled and toppled over, landing on her bottom. The ball sailed over her head.

"Get off!" Bella spluttered, laughing as her little dog Pepper put his paws round her neck and tried to lick her face. "Your breath stinks!"

Louie jogged over. "It's not his breath," he said. "Pepper's rolled in something smelly."

"Yuck!" Bella wrinkled her nose and pushed Pepper off. She loved Pepper, but not when he rolled in things.

"You looked funny," Louie sniggered. "Landing on your bum like that!"

"It was a bad throw," Bella told him. She got up and brushed down her jeans. "How was I supposed to catch it?"

"Haven't you ever heard of jumping?" Louie asked. "Oh, I forgot. Girls can't jump."

"Come back here and say that again!"

Bella chased Louie, laughing. Barking with excitement, Pepper followed her.

Chestnut Park was shaped like a large triangle. On one side were the backs of the shops and houses on the street where Bella and Louie

lived. On another side was a busy road that Bella and Louis knew not to play near. On the third side was a row of much bigger houses, with large gardens and high hedges separated from the park by a stretch of woodland. Pepper loved the woods. Bella guessed that was where he'd found the stinky stuff to roll in.

Louie was running towards the trees. It was downhill part of the way. Bella ran faster, determined to catch him. At the last minute, Louie swerved. Bella couldn't stop. She toppled into the straggly ditch that separated the woods from Chestnut Park. There was a nasty squelch as she sank into the thick brown mud. Somewhere out of sight, she could hear Louie laughing like a hyena.

"That is so gross!" Bella

squealed, staring in

dismay at the gunge

on her knees and

arms.

Pepper put his head

through the tall grass on the top of the ditch.

One of his ears pricked up and he started

barking wildly.

"Be quiet, Pepper," Bella grumbled, trying to

rub the dirt off.

Pepper barked again, running up and down.

His eyes were fixed on something near Bella.

Bella saw what looked like a large lump of mud

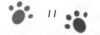

lying in the ditch. The lump got on to four legs and waved a long mucky tail at her.

"Louie, come quickly!" Bella shouted.

Louie's eyes almost popped out of his head. "It's a mud monster!" he shouted.

"Woof!" Pepper barked, almost beside himself.

"Don't be silly," said Bella. "It's a *dog*. The poor thing must have fallen in the ditch and it couldn't get out again!"

The dog was so caked in mud that it was having trouble opening its eyes. Louie kept a safe distance as Bella cautiously reached out her hand. The dog sniffed her fingers.

"Steady now," said Bella gently. "I'm not going to hurt you."

The dog's tail waved again. It was breathing quite fast, like it was in shock. Bella climbed up the bank. The dog tried to follow, but scrabbled and slid back down. It wasn't wearing a collar. Bella reached down and grabbed its muddy scruff. It was a big dog, and it was heavy. She wasn't sure she could pull it out. But she was determined to try.

The dog panted hard. Its sides were heaving.

Bella dug her heels in and pulled. Scrabbling and whining, the dog tried to climb the bank again. This time, it succeeded. It jumped clumsily up at Bella and licked her. This made Bella even muddier, but she didn't care.

Pepper growled and hid behind Louie as the exhausted dog flopped down on the grass. Bella looked around for the dog's owner. Apart from her and Louie, there was no one else in Chestnut Park.

"Where did it come from?" Louie asked, coming a little closer.

"Mud Monster Land," said Bella, rolling her eyes. "Oh, and thanks for all your help. I couldn't have done it without you."

"I didn't know it was a dog, did I?" Louie muttered. "It looked scary."

"Let's take it back to Mum," said Bella. "We can wash it at Dream Dogs."

She felt a little skip in her stomach at the thought of her mum's dog parlour. Dream Dogs was Bella's favourite place, with its pink walls and hanging plants and the smell of wet dog in the air. Washing the muck off to find out what kind of dog they'd found would be really exciting.

"Mum won't let you wash it in Dream Dogs," Louie said. "It's too dirty."

"That's what Dream Dogs is *for*," Bella pointed out. "Washing dogs. Remember?"

Bella teased Louie about mud monsters all the

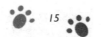

way back across Chestnut Park. The strange dog followed Bella adoringly. Pepper pressed himself close to Louie's heels and growled every few steps.

"Pepper still thinks it's a monster," Louie said as they turned into their street.

"He's just jealous," Bella said.

It did look like Pepper was jealous. As soon as Bella unlatched the dog-gate between the door of Dream Dogs and the parlour, he trotted to his basket and lay down with his back to Bella.

"Mum!" Bella said. "You'll never guess what we found!"

Bella and Louie's mum Suzi looked up from where she was drying a little white West

Highland terrier. Her eyes widened.

"It's a dog," said Bella proudly.

"Take it out before it—" Suzi began.

The rest of her words were lost as the muddy dog shook itself. Bella shrieked. Louie yelled. Suzi ducked. And mud went *everywhere*.

Two

Gold!

"BELLA!" Suzi groaned, staring at the Westie on her drying table. His fluffy white coat was covered in mud. "Now I'll have to wash Angus again! You know better than to bring a wet dog inside that hasn't shaken itself."

Louie giggled.

"Oops," Bella said, biting her lip. "Sorry."

The muddy dog flopped on to the floor, adding to the mess. Suzi winced.

"I'll wash the floor, Mum," Bella said quickly. "And the walls, and whatever got dirty. But please can we wash this dog after Angus? It fell in the ditch in Chestnut Park and it hasn't got a collar and I couldn't see an owner and—"

The Dream Dog door tinkled open, interrupting Bella.

"Whatever happened?" exclaimed the old lady in the doorway. "Did you know there's mud on the ceiling, Suzi?"

"Sorry, Miss Waldicott," said Suzi. "We all just had a little... *accident*. I'll have to give Angus a

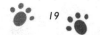

fresh rinse. I hope you're not in a hurry."

Miss Waldicott perched on the seat beneath the window. "No plans this morning," she said. "I'm visiting my sister Grace this afternoon. She moved into Meadowbanks last month but she is finding it a bit hard to settle in, so I like to try and visit as much as I can."

"The nursing home?" asked Suzi, lifting Angus back into the bath tub.

Miss Waldicott nodded. "It's a lovely place — delicious home-made cakes," she said. She leaned forward confidingly. "But I think Grace is missing her own little flat on the seafront and hasn't spoken a word since she moved in. I'm sure she'll be very happy at Meadowbanks but it might just take a little time for her to get used to her new surroundings."

Suzi looked up from the bath. "It's hard moving somewhere new, but I'm sure she's in good hands."

Bella pulled the muddy dog back on to its feet. "I suppose we'd better take you outside," she said.

"You can bring her back when I've finished Angus," Suzi called as Bella pushed open the back door. "Louie? Get some food and water. That animal must be hungry. Then we can wash her and you can tell me the whole story from the beginning. And on the subject of washing, Bella, go and change your clothes and wash your face and hands. You look nearly as bad as the dog! I'm so sorry, Miss Waldicott..."

The dog lay down on her side in the yard. She was still panting hard. The mud on her head had dried now, and the fur was hard and matted.

"So you're a girl, are you?" Bella said. "We'll give you a name as soon as we've washed you."

The strange dog was bigger than Pepper, with triangular ears that flopped down and a square muzzle. Her coat looked thick, and she was very broad across her back and tummy. Bella guessed that her tail would be plumey and gorgeous once they washed it. But what was she? Bella wondered, as she headed upstairs to change. A collie? A Labrador?

When Bella came back, the dog still hadn't touched the food that Louie had put down for her.

"She looked like she'd been in that ditch for ages," Bella said, watching as the dog paced around the yard. "I thought she'd be hungry. Why isn't she eating?"

"Bella!" Suzi called from inside the salon. "Amber's here!"

Bella ran inside to see her best friend. Amber's long hair was loose on her shoulders today, instead of tied up in plaits the way it usually was.

"Thank you, Suzi, dear!" Miss Waldicott was saying as she left with a freshly washed and dried Angus tucked under her arm.

Bella grabbed Amber's arm as the salon door swung shut behind Miss Waldicott. "You've got to see this!" she said, towing Amber out of the back door.

"Is it a dog?" Amber asked, staring at the muddy beast panting in the sunshine.

Bella nodded. "Of course it is!" she said in excitement. "Do you want to help wash her?"

Amber's eyes gleamed. "Definitely!"

"Has she eaten anything?" Suzi asked as Bella and Amber led the dog back into the salon.

Louie shook his head.

"Oh well," Suzi said. "Perhaps she'll feel like something after her bath."

Bella and Amber coaxed the muddy dog up the steps and into the bath. Pepper stared grumpily at Bella from his basket. Bella blew him a kiss as her mum handed her the shower attachment. She'd make it up to Pepper later.

"Here goes," said Bella.

She directed the water at the dog's back. Mud poured off.

"We're going to block the plughole," Amber gasped as rivers of brown gloop ran off the dog's legs and back. "Hey, don't sit down... We need to clean your tummy!"

Slowly, the water began to run clear. Bella fetched the shampoo. She and Amber rubbed it in. More mud cascaded down the plughole.

"What colour is she?" Amber said, peering at the dog's wet back after ten minutes of scrubbing.

Bella ruffled up the dog's fur as Suzi turned off the water. It gleamed beneath her fingers.

"Gold," she breathed. "She's a golden retriever, Amber! And she's *gorgeous*!"

Three

A Very Big Surprise!

The clean golden retriever sat patiently as Bella and Amber took turns with Suzi's big dog-dryer. She kept trying to lie down, but Bella coaxed her up again so she could dry her all over.

"Look how bright she is now," Amber said, switching off the dryer at last and ruffling up the retriever's silky fur. "She's like a big golden nugget."

"Nugget!" Bella exclaimed. "That's what we should call her!"

Nugget panted and wriggled as Amber and Bella kissed her and stroked her silky golden ears. Her shoulders and ribs felt bony, making Bella wonder when she'd last eaten. It was funny that her tummy was so fat.

"She's probably got a name already," Suzi warned, washing away the mud around the rim of the bath. "It's been quite a day for her, but tomorrow I must take her to the vet so that they can check if she has a microchip. Then we'll know if she belongs to anyone. We'll also need to alert the police, or put up posters. Someone might be missing her."

"We'll do posters," Bella said. "Can we borrow your computer and printer, Mum? And your camera?"

Suzi fetched her digital camera out of the drawer beneath the till and handed it to Bella. Bella snapped a picture of Nugget.

"We'll make you a brilliant poster, Nugget," she promised, lowering the camera. "Come on, Amber. We'll do it upstairs!"

Bella and Amber spent a happy half-hour designing a poster for Nugget on Suzi's computer. They dropped in the photo Bella had taken, and put LOST! GOLDEN RETRIEVER! in

big red letters right across the top. At the bottom they put the Dream Dogs address and phone number.

"I made you sandwiches," said Suzi. "You can take them with you if you're keen to get the posters up around Sandmouth. And don't forget – you'll need something to put the posters up with!"

Happily eating their sandwiches, Bella and Amber clattered downstairs. Their posters were tucked into two supermarket bags alongside a wodge of sticky-tack, a roll of tape and a little box of drawing pins. Pepper barked forlornly from his basket. Bella ran over and kissed him.

"You've had your walk, Pepper," she said. "Be nice to Nugget now, won't you?" Nugget lifted her big golden head from where she had been sniffing at the salon's airing cupboard and panted at Bella and Amber as they closed the door behind them.

It took Bella and Amber nearly two hours to put up all the posters.

"I'm starving," Amber announced as Bella stuck up the last poster on the noticeboard at their school, Cliffside Primary. "Has your mum got biscuits?"

Chattering and laughing, Bella and Amber strolled back to Dream Dogs. There was a light wind blowing in over the sea as they walked up the beach, ruffling the sand and making the brightly coloured posters along the seafront flutter in the breeze.

"I hope Nugget's owner sees one of our posters soon," said Bella as they turned into her street. She remembered the horrible sick feeling she'd had when they'd lost Pepper. "It's awful, losing your dog."

Amber spread her arms. "They can't miss them!" she joked. "We put a poster up on every tree, lamp-post, telegraph pole and letter box in Sandmouth!"

Bella pushed open the door to Dream Dogs.

"We're back!" she called, looking around the empty salon. "Mum? Louie? Is anyone here?"

Suzi came into the salon. She had a funny look on her face. "You'll never believe what's just happened, girls," she said. She glanced at the tall airing cupboard where she kept the Dream Dogs' clean towels and washing products.

"Someone's claimed Nugget already?" Bella asked.

"That was quick!" said Amber in surprise.

Suzi shook her head. "I should have guessed the minute I saw Nugget," she said. "I feel very stupid."

"You're not making sense, Mum," said Bella. "Nugget's all right, isn't she?"

Suzi laughed. "Oh yes," she said. "She's fine. If you take a look in there, you'll see just how fine."

She nodded at the cupboard. Feeling puzzled,

Curled up on a pile of towels at the bottom of the cupboard lay Nugget. But not just Nugget. Resting his head on Nugget's back lay Pepper.

And snuggled up to Nugget's belly were two squirming, furry bundles. Nugget looked up at Bella and panted. If dogs could smile, Nugget was grinning from ear to ear.

"Ohmigosh!" Amber squealed. "Nugget's had PUPPIES!"

A Big Responsibility

"Thanks so much for coming to check on Nugget and the puppies, Jane" Suzi called, as Sandmouth's vet walked to her car, parked outside the Dream Dogs salon. As the car door slammed and the little blue Mini pulled away, Suzi turned to Bella and Amber, who were bent over Nugget, looking adoringly at the two golden puppies curled up asleep next to their very proud-looking mum.

Jane had given both the puppies and Nugget a thorough examination and had told Bella both mum and babies were fighting fit. "Healthy as a horse!" she had declared and Louie had giggled and whispered to Bella, "Duh! Doesn't she know they are dogs? Where did she learn to be a vet?" Bella had poked him in the ribs and sssshh'd him and Suzi had given him The Look. Little brothers could be so annoying.

Nugget was exhausted after being stuck in the ditch but Jane said she just needed lots of rest and time with her pups so they could 'bond',

which Jane explained was very important because mum and pups needed to get to know each other. The vet had also given Suzi lots of advice about looking after very young puppies and had even lent her a book that she had brought with her from her practice. Bella couldn't wait to start reading it so she could learn everything there was to know about newborn dogs and the best way to look after them. Jane had warned Suzi that taking on the care of Nugget and her puppies was a huge responsibility. Bella was absolutely determined that she would spend every minute she could helping her mum, if it meant they could keep the puppies at Dream Dogs.

"Well then, seeing as Jane says Nugget hasn't got a microchip," said Suzi, reaching over the Dream Dogs counter to take the pink cordless phone from the counter, "we need to call the animal rescue centre and get some advice."

Bella sat with her back to the counter, with Pepper cuddled in her lap. She buried her face into his fuzzy coat and squeezed  her eyes shut. *What if the rescue centre thinks we don't know enough about puppies to keep them here? What if they decide to take over the responsibility of finding Nugget's owner?* Bella's tummy gave a nervous little flip as she thought how awful it would be if they turned up in their van and took Nugget and the puppies away. Even though she was trying not to listen, she could hear her mum on the phone, talking to someone from the centre. Every so often Bella caught an "Oh, yes, absolutely" or an "I completely understand" and tried hard not to guess what her mum was saying to the person on the other end of the phone.

After what seemed like a year, Bella heard Suzi return the pink cordless telephone to its cradle on the counter. Knowing she couldn't put off hearing what the rescue centre had to say any longer, she took a deep breath, gave Pepper a squeeze for good luck and looked up at her mum.

Suzi was smiling broadly. "Well, you needn't look so glum, love, it's good news!"

Bella let out a big whoosh of breath that she hadn't realised she'd been holding in and waited for her mum to speak.

"I spoke to the head of the re-homing team and told him all about Dream Dogs. I mentioned Pepper and explained that I've got heaps of experience looking after dogs of all shapes and sizes and that I would have a very enthusiastic helper if the animal centre did allow us to keep the puppies here."

Realising Suzi was referring to her as the helper, Bella nodded her head vigorously and tried to look as grown-up and responsible as she could.

"So," Suzi continued, taking a big breath, "we can look after Nugget and the puppies while we try to find Nugget's owner. But, the man I spoke to thinks that may be impossible as she wasn't microchipped and had no collar on when you found her. So, they've agreed to give us seven weeks, until after the puppies have been weaned, to find homes for them all. If we haven't been able to home them by the end of the seven weeks, they will be taken to the animal rescue centre in Billington and re-homed from there."

Bella knew that the big town of Billington was over forty miles away, so the chances of ever seeing Nugget or her puppies again were very low. Suddenly Bella felt like there was a heavy weight sitting on her shoulders and she knew it wouldn't go away until they had found new homes for Nugget and her puppies in Sandmouth.

Seven weeks was a long time, but they had a lot to do...

Five

Puppy Fun

"Are the puppies getting bigger?" Amber asked breathlessly. "Are they walking yet? Oh, please, Bella – can I come over after school?"

Bella laughed. "Yes times three," she said. "Mum's got so used to having you round for tea over the last three weeks that she automatically makes extra food. Does your mum remember what you look like?"

"It's Nugget's fault for having such beautiful puppies," Amber said. "I still can't believe it, really."

Neither could Bella. She had watched them from blind bundles to bright-eyed, silky-eared baby dogs over the past three weeks, and she still felt like she was dreaming. The special puppy smell made her want to jump for joy every time she smelled it. Dream Dogs had never had so many customers either. Everyone wanted a peep at Nugget and her two pups. Pepper had got very protective since the puppies had arrived, and growled at anyone who got too close. Bella

had to keep putting him outside.

"So they're walking?" Amber asked. "Which one did it first? I bet it was Sandy. He's bigger."

Bella shook her head. "It wasn't," she said. "It was Buttercup."

Amber looked amazed. "But Buttercup's so much smaller!"

"And the most determined," Bella said. "You should have seen her, Amber. She got up and wobbled across the floor like she was on ice skates. She barged Sandy out of the way! But as soon as Sandy realised that she was leaving the cupboard, he immediately tried to follow and fell over on his fat little bottom!"

Amber's eyes went misty. "Ah! It's so sweet

that they do everything together. They are totally inseparable."

"I know! That's why it's so important that we find someone who can adopt them both. They would be so miserable if they couldn't be re-homed together," Bella said, a frown wrinkling her forehead.

Amber sighed. "I *wish* I could take them home," she said, like she had every day for the past three weeks.

Mr Evans, Bella's teacher, stopped at Amber and Bella's table. Amber and Bella stopped talking and looked at him guiltily. Were they in trouble?

"How are the puppies, Bella?" Mr Evans asked.

Bella giggled. Somehow, the arrival of the puppies had changed Mr Evans's normal classroom rule about talking in lessons. "They're fine, Mr Evans," she said. "You can come and see them if you like."

"I've booked Barney in for a wash with your mum at the weekend," said Mr Evans. "Perhaps I can see them then."

Mr Evans's dog Barney was a golden retriever like Nugget. He was bigger than Nugget though, and a darker colour.

"You'll have to find homes for them soon," Amber told Bella as Mr Evans moved away. "Otherwise the RSPCA will have to take them in, and Nugget too, and if they can't find homes for them in Sandmouth, we'll never see them again."

Bella pulled a face. "I know," she said. "I wish they could stay with us forever."

"Still nothing from our posters?" Amber asked.

Bella shook her head. After three weeks, no one had claimed Nugget yet and she was starting to worry that no one ever would.

Mr Evans was Dream Dogs's first customer on Saturday morning.

"Morning!" he said, peering around the salon. "How are the pups, then?"

"Getting big," said Suzi. She helped Mr Evans take off Barney's lead. "They'll be on to solids next week."

"They're in the cupboard if you want a look," Bella explained.

"The cupboard?" Mr Evans repeated, looking surprised.

"It's where she gave birth," Suzi said. "We've done everything we can to coax her into a basket, but Nugget refuses to move. So we've stopped trying."

Bella took Pepper out of the cupboard before he could growl at Mr Evans. She stroked Pepper's ears as Mr Evans exclaimed over Nugget and her pups.

"Adorable!" he said. "Can I touch them?"

"Of course you can," said Suzi as she helped Barney up the steps and into the bath tub.

"It's good for puppies to be touched," Bella said. "Just be careful with the smaller one. She's called Buttercup, and she—"

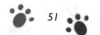

"Ow!" Mr Evans yelped, pulling his finger away.

"—nips," Bella finished with a grin.

Both the puppies were confident on their feet now. With their stumpy legs and tails that were a bit too long, they were really funny to watch. Bella and Louie spent a lot of time picking them up from different corners of the salon and returning them to the cupboard.

Mr Evans stroked Nugget behind the ears.

"Clever mum," he said. "I can see where your babies get their looks from. Retrievers are the best dogs in the world." He glanced up at Pepper, who was wriggling in Bella's arms. "No offence, Pepper," he added.

Suzi soaped, rinsed and dried Barney carefully. He was a magnificent dog. Nugget watched from her cupboard as Suzi dried Barney's tummy and brushed his coat until it gleamed.

"Perhaps we'll see you walking out in Chestnut Park soon, Nugget," said Mr Evans. "You and your babies. What a sight that would be!"

"It certainly would," Suzi said to Bella as Mr Evans and Barney left the salon. "Buttercup would nip everyone and Sandy would sit down in the middle of

the field and have to be carried home and... Oh! heavens, Buttercup's halfway up the stairs!"

"We'll have to build them a run out in the yard soon," said Bella, scooping Buttercup up. She kissed the tiny puppy before putting her back with Nugget, and breathed in her special puppy smell.

"We'll have to find them new homes too," Suzi said. "We can't get too attached, Bella."

The puppies wriggled and yipped as they latched on to feed. They were so unbelievably wonderful.

"It's too late, Mum," Bella sighed. "I *am* attached."

Giving Nugget and the puppies up was going to be the hardest thing she'd ever had to do.

Six

Sophie

When Bella went into her classroom on Monday, a new girl was standing beside Mr Evans. She was small and had black hair plaited in rows down her head.

"This is Sophie Olowu," said Mr Evans. Sophie stared at the ground. "Sophie's mother has just taken over as manager of Meadowbanks — the nursing home on Hamilton Road."

Bella frowned at the mention of Meadowbanks. It was familiar. Then she remembered. Miss Waldicott's sister Grace had gone to live at Meadowbanks.

"They have home-made cakes," she said, remembering something Miss Waldicott had said.

The class laughed, and Bella blushed. She hadn't meant to say that out loud.

"Since you know it, Bella," said Mr Evans, "perhaps you could look after Sophie today. Amber? Move up and make some room for Sophie, will you?"

"We only moved to Sandmouth a couple of months ago," Bella said chattily as Sophie put her things down on their table. "It's great, being by the sea."

"Mr Evans is a good teacher," Amber added. "You'll like him."

Sophie fiddled with her pens but didn't say anything.

"What was your last school like?" Bella asked.

The new girl stayed silent.

"What about your family?" Amber said. "Have you got any brothers or sisters?"

Sophie shook her head very slightly.

"Any pets?" Bella asked.

Sophie shook her head again.

"You don't say much, do you?" said Amber cheerfully.

Sophie looked embarrassed.

"You'll get used to Big-Mouth here," Bella said, rolling her eyes at Amber. "She talks more than the whole class put together."

"I do not!" Amber protested.

"Enough chattering, Amber!" Mr Evans called. "Time for registration!"

By the end of the day, Sophie still hadn't said anything. Every time Bella asked her a question, Sophie either shook her head or stared at the floor. It was hard work. But Bella knew what it was like, being the new girl in class. So she kept smiling at her, and hoped that Sophie would soon feel brave enough to smile back.

Suzi was at the gates when Bella, Amber and Sophie came out of class into the warm spring sunshine. She was standing beside a tall lady that Bella guessed was Sophie's mum.

"Hi, love!" Suzi waved enthusiastically. "This is Mrs Olowu. She's new in Sandmouth. Since we know all about that, we've been having a lovely chat." Suzi smiled at Sophie. "And you must be Sophie," she said.

Sophie ducked her head, clutching on to her books.

"Sophie is very shy," said Mrs Olowu apologetically.

"Never mind," said Suzi. She gave Bella a hug. "Mrs Olowu's invited us over for tea at Meadowbanks this afternoon," she said. "That's nice, isn't it?"

Bella wasn't sure how she felt about going for tea at Sophie's. Trying to be friendly and not getting any kind of response was really tiring. And she'd been looking forward to fussing over Nugget's puppies.

"OK," she said cautiously.

"Brilliant," said Suzi. "Louie's going home with

his friend James tonight, so we can all be girls together."

"Woof!" Pepper said, and started frisking around Bella's legs.

"Apart from Pepper," Bella reminded her mum.

Sophie reached out her hand and stroked Pepper's head. Thrilled at the extra attention, Pepper jumped up. To Bella's astonishment, Sophie burst out laughing. It was the first sound Bella had heard Sophie make. It was lovely – like a big, happy explosion.

They walked together, away from the school and up the hill towards Hamilton Road. Sophie had stopped laughing, and was quiet again. Bella

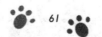

didn't try to talk to her. She just listened to her mum and Mrs Olowu chatting. Then she saw Sophie glancing sideways at Pepper, who was bouncing along beside her on his lead.

"You can hold the lead if you want," Bella said.

Sophie's face lit up. She took Pepper's lead and ran up the road ahead of Bella, turning up the drive of a big blue house. MEADOWBANKS, said a large yellow sign on the gate. CARING FOR YOUR LOVED ONES. Bella guessed that the windows at the front had views of the sea, while the ones at the back looked over the woods and into Chestnut Park.

"Take Bella into the garden, will you, Sophie?"

said Mrs Olowu. "We will bring out some tea."

Bella followed Sophie and Pepper round the side of the house, to a large lawned garden. A few Meadowbanks residents sat on garden benches, enjoying the sunshine. Bella wondered if one of them was Miss Waldicott's sister.

Pepper was straining at the lead.

"Let him off if you want," Bella suggested.

Pepper took off like a rocket, his brown tail wagging like mad. One of the residents on a nearby bench laughed. So did Sophie.

"You've got a great laugh," said Bella.

Sophie spoke so softly that Bella almost missed it. "Pepper's funny," she said.

"You can say that again," Bella agreed.

They both watched as Pepper zoomed round a big tree near the back of the garden like his paws were on fire. Sophie choked on a giggle.

"Pepper's funny," she repeated.

"Hey," said Bella. "Was that a joke? Because I said 'You can say that again'?"

Sophie gave another of her throaty laughs and didn't answer.

"We've got puppies at home," Bella said impulsively. "Would you like to come and see them some time?"

Sophie's face split into a huge smile. "Really?" she said. "Oh yes. Yes, please!"

Seven

An Idea...

By the end of the week, Bella had learned a little more about Sophie. She missed her old school, and her old house. But most of all, she missed her best friend Lucy and Lucy's little dog, Jingle.

"Jingle was a black and white mongrel," Sophie told Bella as they walked down the beach towards Dream Dogs on Friday afternoon. "She had short legs and the longest tail you ever saw. She was really gentle. Me, Lucy and Jingle did everything together."

"You must really miss them," Bella said.

Sophie looked sad and nodded. "I used to go over to Lucy's after school and we would spend hours brushing Jingle and making her look like a show dog," she said. "Then we'd go to the park and Jingle would trot around on her lead like she was in the judging ring. I'm sure she was showing off!"

"It must have been really hard for you to have said goodbye to Jingle when you moved to Sandmouth," Bella guessed. She glanced at

Pepper, who was digging madly by the beach huts. "I can't imagine not having Pepper."

Pepper looked up. His nose was covered in sand. It made Bella laugh. Sophie smiled, her sadness briefly forgotten.

"You'd like another dog," Bella asked, a glimmer of a plan forming in her mind. "Wouldn't you?"

Sophie shrugged and stared at the sand. "Mum would say no," she said.

"She loves dogs but I suppose she can't really have a puppy running around a nursing home, can she?"

Bella didn't reply. She was too busy thinking how nice it would be if there *was* a dog at Meadowbanks, and that if *she* was a resident, it would be lovely to have a cute little puppy scampering around the place.

The curly pink Dream Dogs sign shone brightly as Suzi opened the door to the salon. Louie charged in, jumping over the dog-fence with a yell. Sophie hung back behind Bella, staring around in wonder.

"This is brilliant," she said. She reached out and touched the photos on the Dream Dogs

pinboard. "Who are all these dogs?"

"Mum's customers," Bella explained. "People give us snaps of their dogs, and we put them up. Come on. The puppies are over here."

Suzi had built an indoor pen for Nugget and her pups at the back of the salon. The pen was low enough for Nugget to climb in and out whenever she wanted — but not low enough for the puppies to escape.

The two puppies were standing with their front paws on the top of the pen. Buttercup barked, and Sandy whined. Scrabbling madly with her back paws, brave little Buttercup tried to climb over, but fell back with a tiny woof. The puppies' tails waved happily as Sophie sank to

her knees and reached out her hands.

"Beautiful," Sophie whispered. She stroked Buttercup and tickled Sandy behind his ears. "You're the luckiest person in the world, Bella!"

"I know," Bella said proudly.

Sophie picked them both up and cuddled them to her cheeks. Pepper licked Nugget hello. Much to Bella's relief, he'd stopped growling every time someone got too close to the puppies.

"I wish I could have them," Sophie said. "I really, really wish I could."

"We really do need a home for them, but it's trying to find someone who is willing to take both," Suzi said. "I've had several customers offering to take one but I just can't bear to separate them. Then she added hopefully, "perhaps you should ask your mum, Sophie?"

Sophie buried her nose in Buttercup's tummy and didn't say anything.

"Mrs Olowu doesn't want a dog, let alone two," Bella explained to her mum.

Suzi looked disappointed. "Oh," she said. "Well, I can understand that. Taking on a puppy is a big commitment and having two is double the work. I'm just so determined to find someone who wants them both, otherwise the RSPCA will take over the job of re-homing them and we might never see them again." Suzi stopped suddenly and pulled her face into a smile. "Come on, let's be positive! Perhaps you and Sophie would like to make another poster, Bella? I'll put an ad in next week's paper as well."

Although she tried not to let it, Bella's heart sank. Her mum was right. They were running out of time. The RSPCA had been really kind to let Bella and her mum try to find homes for Nugget and her puppies in Sandmouth, but it was beginning to feel like they would have to let the RSPCA come and take them away.

"My Nugget poster didn't work, did it?" she pointed out. "No one's come to claim her."

"Someone will eventually," said Suzi. "I'm sure of it."

Nugget and the puppies have *to stay in Sandmouth*, Bella thought to herself as she gave Nugget a cuddle. *If the RSPCA took them, we'd never see them out on the beach, or at Chestnut Park. It would be like they never came to Dream Dogs.*

Bella shook her head as if she was trying to get rid of those awful thoughts from her mind. It was simple, she HAD to find a way to keep

Buttercup and Sandy together and find homes for them all in Sandmouth, but the big question was...

HOW?

Eight

What Plan?!

Bella had strange dreams that night, about puppies covered in cake mixture running around Meadowbanks with her mum chasing after them in a cook's apron, waving a wooden spoon. She was glad when the sun rose, and she sat up in bed, smiling at her wacky dream.

And then suddenly the idea that had formed earlier in Bella's head popped like a bubble to the surface. It wasn't just Sophie who loved dogs. One of the residents at Meadowbanks had really laughed at Pepper the other day. Wouldn't two little puppies be just what Meadowbanks needed? Perhaps if Mrs Olowu thought it would be nice for the residents as well as Sophie, she might think differently about having a dog, especially if Sophie and Bella and her mum helped to train and look after the puppies as much as they could.

Bella leaped out of bed and bounded down the stairs to the kitchen like an excited puppy. Her mum and Louie were already there. Suzi was clutching a cup of coffee.

"Mum?" Bella said, trying to sound calmer than she felt. "Do you think we could take the puppies round to Meadowbanks for the residents to see? I'm sure they'd love them."

"What a lovely idea," Suzi said. "I'll just finish my coffee then I'll call Mrs Olowu."

Bella grinned secretly to herself. She was determined that Meadowbanks should have two new residents. And once Mrs Olowu saw how gorgeous they were, how could she say no?

Bella had just got to the good part of making her bed – arranging her collection of stuffed toys, which were mainly all dogs, on her pillow, when she heard Suzi call her name from the stairs.

"Bella! I've just spoken to Mrs Olowu on the phone, and she's agreed that we can take Nugget and the pups over to see the residents this afternoon. Apparently Sophie was thrilled with the idea and said that the puppies could run around the garden."

Bella felt a flicker of excitement. She pushed all of her recent worrying thoughts to the back of her mind and concentrated on her plan to make Mrs Olowu fall in love with the puppies and offer them a home at Meadowbanks. She smiled at the thought — with not one, but two puppies to love and look after, Sophie would be the happiest girl in the world! Perhaps one day she could even

take them to visit Jingle!

"Can we go for

tea?" Louie asked,

breaking Bella from

her daydream. "Miss

Waldicott says—"

"They do home-made cakes, I know," Suzi

said. "Yes. We'll head over there at three o'clock

this afternoon. It'll be a great success. And

fingers crossed your little plan will work too,"

she added, looking sideways at Bella.

"What plan?" Bella asked innocently.

Suzi laughed. She put her coffee cup in the sink

and redid her hair in its long, shiny brown

ponytail. "Come on," she said. "I've got a salon to run. Mr Evans is bringing Barney for a trim at nine-thirty."

Mr Evans had been bringing Barney to the salon a lot recently, Bella realised. Perhaps, if her plan to re-home the puppies at Meadowbanks didn't work, then maybe they could persuade Mr Evans to take them? For the first time in a month, Bella suddenly felt a surge of confidence. Nugget and her pups were going to find homes in Sandmouth – she just knew it.

The little bell above Dream Dogs tinkled and Barney came bounding through into the salon, a ball of dark gold fur and madly wagging tail. On the other end of the lead was a rather hot and dishevelled-looking Mr Evans. Bella wondered with a smile who was taking who for a walk, seeing as Barney had barged past his owner so determinedly to be first into the salon.

"Gosh, I'm sorry about Barney. I don't know what's got into him lately. He dragged me up the road on his lead as if he knew we were coming to Dream Dogs and couldn't wait to get here!"

Well, that answered Bella's question! "Perhaps he's just excited to see the puppies?" Bella asked, stroking Barney's smooth, domed head. "They have probably grown quite a bit since you last saw them. Buttercup's almost caught up with Sandy now, and seeing as they never want to be apart, sometimes I can't tell which one is which!"

But before Mr Evans could respond, Nugget sprung from her bed in the puppy pen and trotted over to Barney, where they stood sniffing gently at each other. Laughing loudly, Suzi put one arm around Bella's shoulders and ruffled Barney's thick coat.

"I'm not so sure it's Buttercup and Sandy he looks forward to seeing, love – it's their beautiful mum. I think he has a crush on Nugget!"

And judging by the way Nugget was wagging her plumed tail and practically smiling at Barney, the feeling was mutual!

Nine

Meadowbanks

"The residents are so excited," said Mrs Olowu as she opened the door. Sophie peeped round from behind her mother. "This was a lovely idea, Bella."

"Let's see if we can tempt you to home these two while we're here, shall we?" Suzi joked, opening the back of the Dream Dogs mini van. The two puppies yipped with excitement from their fleece-lined travel cage and sniffed the strange new air.

"Yes, Mrs Olowu!" Bella said at once. "I know Sophie would look after them."

"I would, Mum. You wouldn't have to do anything!" said Sophie hopefully.

Mrs Olowu shook her head. "What *would* the residents say?" she declared, with a half-smile. "Please – bring the puppies round the back. Everyone is waiting."

The sun was out, and so were the Meadowbanks residents and their nurses, together with a few visitors and a table groaning

with cakes and sandwiches. Bella recognised one
of the visitors straight away.

"Bella!" said Miss Waldicott
with a wave. "Suzi! Louie!
What a lovely surprise
this is! Grace, dear?
These are the people
from Dream Dogs – Angus's
hairdressers, you might say!"

The frail old lady beside Miss Waldicott didn't
seem to hear. Her pale blue eyes were looking
somewhere far away, and her tiny hands were
folded in her lap. Tied to one of the bench legs,
Angus barked and wagged his stumpy white tail
at the sight of Bella. Bella fussed over him while

Pepper sniffed Angus's bottom, making Louie giggle.

"Have some tea," suggested Miss Waldicott. "Grace likes the iced buns, don't you, dear?"

The old lady's far-away eyes focused on something. Bella turned to see Sandy and Buttercup romping with Sophie down the middle of the lawn.

"The puppies are lovely, aren't they?" Bella said, smiling at the old lady.

"That's the thing, Bella, dear," said Miss Waldicott, looking pleased. "Chat to Grace. She doesn't chat back, but—"

"Lovely."

Miss Waldicott almost dropped the iced bun

she was putting on a plate. "What did you say, dear?" she asked.

"Lovely," said the old lady again.

"Well I never!" cried Miss Waldicott. "That's the first time Grace has spoken since she's been here! All because of those two!" she laughed, pointing to the pups who were now frisking around the legs of the bench. "Bless my stars!"

Hearing Miss Waldicott's exclamation, Mrs Olowu turned to see what was happening.

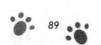

"It was the puppies," Bella grinned. "They're very good for the residents, Mrs Olowu. You can see for yourself!"

Louie and Sophie were trying to catch the pups as they ran around, with Pepper barking encouragement. With the help of the nurses, they brought them over for the Meadowbanks residents to stroke. Several of the old ladies laughed as they sank their fingers into the puppies' soft fur.

Cuddling Buttercup, Sophie plopped Sandy into her mother's arms.

"Oh!" said Mrs Olowu. She looked down at Sandy's round golden face. "He's adorable!"

After a while she gently placed the puppy back

down on the lawn and immediately he went bounding off after Buttercup. The pups raced side by side until they collapsed in a squeaking, furry bundle in the grass by a small group of residents, who all laughed and clapped their hands in delight. Nugget, contented that her pups were safe and happy, trotted off towards the big hedge at the end of the garden that backed on to the wood.

"I would look after them, Mum," Sophie was saying as Bella rejoined the others. "And look at how much the residents love them."

Mrs Olowu was now looking at the pups, who were cuddled up together so snugly, you couldn't tell where Buttercup ended and Sandy began.

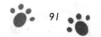

There was a strange look on her face.

"They love it here already, Mrs Olowu," Bella said. Surely their gorgeousness would change Mrs Olowu's mind?

"This place needs a puppy," said one of the nurses.

The residents nodded and murmured to each other.

"It's cheered me up no end..."

"I haven't laughed so much in ages!"

Mrs Olowu scrunched up her eyes. When she opened them again, Bella knew they'd won. But had she convinced Mrs Olowu enough to take both of them? Bella didn't have time to worry over this, as Mrs Olowu's next words took even Bella by surprise.

"I know how lonely it can be moving somewhere new and leaving everyone you know and love behind. So there's no way we can split Buttercup and Sandy up. We can't just have one," she said. "I'm assuming you would be happy if we took them both?"

Sophie gave a gasp and threw her arms round her mum's waist. Bella could hear her muffled voice saying, "Thank you, thank you, thank you," over and over again. Then she rushed over to the sleeping puppies and covered both Buttercup and

Sandy in kisses. Pepper barked and started chasing his tail.

"They'll be ready to leave their mum in two weeks," Suzi smiled. "Are you going to change their names?"

"No," said Sophie, hugging Buttercup so hard that the puppy squeaked. "They're perfect the way they are."

Bella looked around for Nugget. She frowned when she couldn't see her. Then she looked under the bushes and behind the big tree Pepper had sprinted around earlier in the week.

"Nugget!" she called. "Where are you?"

She'd reached the bottom of the garden. The gate was fastened securely. Panicking, Bella stared out into the little patch of woodland that separated Chestnut Park from the houses on Hamilton Street. She glimpsed a flash of gold bounding through the trees towards the park. Bella's heart did a weird sort of swoop as she realised that the flash of gold was Nugget and she was heading straight towards the busy road on the other side of the park!

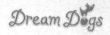

"Mum!" Bella screamed, sprinting back up to the house. "Nugget's got out!"

Suzi gasped.

"I saw her sniffing by the gate earlier," Bella said. "But I checked and the gate was shut tight. She must have slipped through a hole in the fence. We have to catch her before she gets on to the road!"

Ten

After Her!

Bella flew out of the back gate and found herself on the edge of the patch of woodland where she and Louie had first found Nugget. But this time, Nugget was nowhere to be seen. As she desperately scanned the stretch of green that peeked out from between the trees, it was impossible to ignore the road that bordered the other side of the park. A large van hurtled round the sharp bend and whizzed past in a cloud of exhaust fumes, followed closely by two more speeding cars. Bella and Louie knew not to play near that side of the park, but how would Nugget know? Bella knew she had to reach her before something terrible might happen.

Bella could hear her mum calling out and turned round to see her running through the

woods with Pepper at her heels. Sophie, Louie and Mrs Olowu weren't far behind. "She mustn't go near the road!" Bella shouted.

She leaped over the ditch where they'd found Nugget. She dodged through trees and jumped over roots.

"I'm... sure... she'll be all right..." Suzi panted beside Bella. "She's a pretty smart dog..."

Bella plunged on. Pepper raced beside her. Her arms were scratched, and one of her ankles was bleeding. She didn't care. Bursting into the sunshine again, she flung her arms up to shield her eyes. They were in the park. The light was so bright compared to the gloomy woods, for a minute Bella couldn't see a thing. But knowing that every second she wasted, Nugget could be a paw closer to the road, she carried on running.

She ignored the weird spots and stars in her vision... until she felt herself crash into something warm and solid.

"Oooof!" she cried, as two big arms reached out to catch her, stopping her just in time from bouncing back on her bottom on to the grass.

"Goodness, Bella, steady on there!" laughed a familiar voice. "What's the hurry?"

Bella shook the last stars from her eyes and looked up at the man she had bumped into. A man with a large golden retriever sitting at his feet and another one standing meekly beside him. A man she knew very well...

"Mr Evans!"

Bella goggled at her teacher. "You caught Nugget!" she said.

"Well, I can't say there was much catching involved. I recognised Nugget when she burst out of the woods, rather like you just did, but as soon as she saw Barney here, she stopped chasing whatever it was she was chasing and hasn't moved from his side since."

"Woof!" said Barney, nudging Nugget's shoulder with his nose. Nugget nuzzled back joyfully.

"I don't think she was chasing anything," Suzi gasped, who had caught up with Bella and was now standing, bent over, holding her side with both hands. "She was just trying to find Barney!"

By now Louie had reached the park and was staring at Nugget with his mouth open. "That's amazing," he said. "She must have smelled Barney all the way from Meadowbanks and broken out of the garden to come and find him!"

Bella looked at Nugget, who was wagging her tail and looking very guilty at causing Bella so much panic.

Mr Evans eyed Barney, who was licking

Nugget's nose. Nugget's tail wagged furiously.

"Well," he said, "I think that settles it. Nugget

must come and live with us. It would break

Barney's heart if she went somewhere else and we can't have her running off every time she gets a sniff of him."

"Seriously?" Bella gasped.

Mr Evans nodded.

"Nugget and Barney can have more puppies!" Louie shouted.

Mr Evans grinned. "Why not? Then Buttercup and Sandy can have some half-brothers and sisters!" he said.

Bella felt like her face was about to split in half with smiling. Not only did Nugget's puppies have a wonderful new home, Nugget did too and all just around the corner from Dream Dogs!

"Woof!" Pepper barked, and did a long

bottom skid down the park.

"Perfect," Bella sighed happily when everyone

had stopped laughing. "Just *perfect!*"

Top tips from vets!

It can be very difficult to find good homes for puppies, as Bella found out. Getting your dog neutered has important health benefits and means they won't have lots of unwanted babies.

What is neutering?

Neutering is an operation which stops pets from having babies. In females neutering is called 'spaying' and in males it is called 'castration'.

Why is it important?

By getting our pets neutered we can prevent them from developing certain infections and diseases and improves both their quality of and length of life. Neutering is also important to help reduce the problem of stray and unwanted, abandoned pets.

Did you know?

An average dog can have about 12 puppies every year, but it can be much higher than this. Imagine if every female dog in the UK had 16 puppies a year, there just wouldn't be enough people to provide all of them with homes.

For more tips on pet care, great competitions and games visit www.pdsa.org.uk/petprotectors

pdsa
for pets in need of vets

Help PDSA by joining our Pet Protectors Club!

PDSA treats the sick and injured pets of people in need.

For kids who love pets

Members get ...

- Animal year planner
- Membership badge and card
- Cute stickers
- Plus a free bag!
- Personalised fridge magnet
- *Animal Antics* magazine every 2 months

Just £11 a year!

Dream Dogs

CRYSTAL

Crystal might be the most gorgeous, fluffy dog that Bella has ever seen, but she's horribly spoilt. And Crystal's famous owner, Mimi Taylor, is even more demanding!

Bella can't help worrying: will the Dream Dogs pooch parlour be good enough for its most difficult customers ever?

Read on for a sneak preview of the next Dream Dogs adventure...

Bella jumped out of her skin as Louie came charging into the salon from the adjoining flat door.

"Mimi..." he panted. "Mimi's coming... Saw her out of the kitchen window..."

Bella jerked round. Her foot slipped in a puddle of water. She let go of Barney, who bounded down the bath steps with a joyful bark and threw himself at Mr Evans. Suzi shrieked. Mr Evans shouted. Bella went over with an undignified bump on her bottom just as the salon door tinkled and a woman stepped through the door, clutching a tiny little dog in her arms.

Bella gasped for breath. Mimi Taylor's designer sandals tapped over the salon floor towards her.

"Are you OK?" Mimi Taylor asked.

Louie got a fit of the giggles in the corner of the salon. Suzi was trying to wipe Mr Evans's jumper and look at Mimi at the same time, while Mr Evans struggled to get Barney back under control.

"You're Mimi," said Bella stupidly.

Mimi grinned. "Last time I looked, yes," she said.

Take home all of the
Dream Dogs
If you have it, tick it!

Available now:

 ☐

 ☐

Out in May:

 ☐

 ☐

Out in July:

 ☐

 ☐